This book belongs to

....

....

....

First Published 2016 by Ballynafagh Press
This edition published 2019 by Johnny Magory Books
Ballynafagh, Prosperous, Naas, Co. Kildare, Ireland

ISBN: 978-0-9935792-7-1

Text, Illustrations, Design © 2016 Emma-Jane Leeson
www.JohnnyMagory.com

Edited by Aoife Barrett, Dublin, Ireland
Design and Layout by Kim Shaw, Kilkenny, Ireland
Printed in Ireland in KPS Colour Print, Mayo, Ireland
Proud members of Guaranteed Irish

Proud Partners of CMRF Crumlin.
2% of proceeds from the sale of this book will be donated to this charity.
Please visit **www.CMRF.org** for more information.

The Children's Medical
& Research Foundation
Our Lady's Children's
Hospital, Crumlin

Johnny Magory
in the Magical Wild

Emma-Jane Leeson

For Mammy & Daddy
Thanks for the stories

I'll tell you a story about Johnny Magory,
And the adventures he has with his trusty dog Ruairi.

He's a clever boy who's six years old,

He's **usually** good,

but he's

sometimes

bold!

E very morning when Johnny wakes up,

He *slurps* his apple juice from his cup.

He **gobbles** his porridge with

 or

He doesn't mind which - they're both so **yummy**.

A nd when he finishes he licks his lips to say,

"That was **grand** Mammy, Now what'll we do today?"

Every day they do something new,

Like go to the beach or make-and-do.

But today his Mammy

has to clean their house,

And Johnny **can't** stay

as quiet as a mouse.

So into his old

exploring clothes he jumps,

And out to the garden he goes with a bump!

Johnny's faithful dog Ruairi meets him, with a big

wuff!

He'll play for hours, doing all kinds of funny stuff.

As they're disappearing his Mammy gets a hunch,

And quickly shouts,

Don't forget to come in for lunch!

Johnny loses track of time, the same way as his Dad,

But Mammy doesn't like it; it makes her kind of **mad**.

He runs back and kisses her, **promising** he has it timed,

Johnny never means to be late, it just slips his mind!

So off to the bottom of the garden he did bowl,

To his little secret passage down a rabbit hole.

Johnny's hidden tunnel leads into the **magical** wild, where he has special friends who'll only talk to a child.

He knows Mr. Fox, Mrs. Squirrel and their families too,

Johnny's their **only** human friend and they **love** him through and through.

And on the Friday morning when Johnny and Ruairi visit,

He hears his friends cheering, so he shouts out;

What is it?

Mr Badger greets him with his usual friendly grin,

We're having a forest party - come and join in!

Now Johnny **loves** to party; he loves to sing and dance,

He knows he's to be back for lunch but he **can't** miss this chance.

So deeper into the forest they go, Mr. Badger behind,

Until Johnny's sparkling eyes see the BIGGEST party he'll ever find!

Giant frogs are playing silver guitars,

As red squirrels blow horns on pink toy cars.

White swans are plucking golden fiddles,

While grey squirrels sing "Hey Diddle Diddle!"

Hedgehogs are doing mad bomb-dives,

And having the time of their lives,

Splashing into the freezing forest lake,

To cheers from the foxes and the corncrakes!

While Johnny dances for hours with the guys,

Ruairi and the frogs keep doing high fives!

Then Johnny hears a funny noise and he knows...

It's not Ruairi who's singing with the crows.

It's his belly **rumbling** with nothing to munch,

He's played so much he's **missed his lunch!**

He knows he's going to be in trouble -

He feels a bit anxious and in a **muddle.**

Johnny says **Goodbye** to everyone,

Today has been great - the best fun!

Then Ruairi thanks them for all the craic,

And they **run** home to get **quickly** back.

They crawl fast through the secret hole,
With Johnny's clothes as black as coal.

He's heading towards the red back door,
When he hears his Mammy's **big** roar!

Johnny has been very, very bold,
Not doing what he was clearly told.

He said he **meant** to be back on time...

crime!

for his

his room

sent to

...But he's

Later that evening when he's said **sorry** for what he'd done,

Mammy puts him in the bath and *he tells her about the fun...*

From dancing with the **mad** hedgehogs,

And playing **music** with the frogs,

Swimming with the **beautiful** swans,

To waving the fairies' **magic wands!**

Johnny snuggles into his bed,
The day's adventure in his head.

His Mammy kisses him goodnight -

Goodnight Johnny!

And then she turns out the light!

Can you name Johnny Magory's friends?

Why not have your own adventure?

"Johnny Magory in the Magical Wild" was inspired by Ballynafagh Lake near Prosperous in County Kildare, Ireland.

Why not print the free Outdoor Explorer Guide from our website, pack a picnic and take a little explorer on an adventure to try and catch a glimpse of Mr Badger, the swans and all their friends?

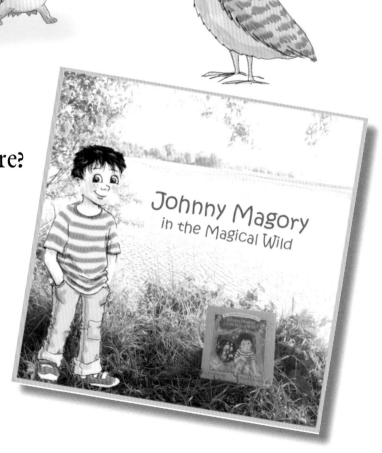